The Story of
Lightning &Thunder

The Story of Lightning & Thunder

Ashley Bryan

A Jean Karl Book
Atheneum 1993 New York
MAXWELL MACMILLAN CANADA
TORONTO
MAXWELL MACMILLAN INTERNATIONAL
NEW YORK   OXFORD   SINGAPORE   SYDNEY

This story is based on *Folk Stories from Southern Nigeria, West Africa*,
by Elphinstone Dayrell (London:
Longmans Green, 1910), 70–71.

*Several steps were taken to make this an environmentally
friendly book. The paper is made from not less than fifty-
percent recycled fibers. The inks used are vegetable oil-based.
Finally, the binders board is one-hundred-percent recycled
material.*

Atheneum   Maxwell Macmillan Canada, Inc.
Macmillan Publishing Company   1200 Eglinton Avenue East
866 Third Avenue   Suite 200
New York, NY 10022   Don Mills, Ontario M3C 3N1

Macmillan Publishing Company is part of the
Maxwell Communication Group of Companies.

First edition
Printed in the United States of America
10   9   8   7   6   5   4   3   2   1
The text of this book is set in Weiss.

Library of Congress Cataloging-in-Publication Data
Bryan, Ashley.
The story of lightning and thunder / Ashley Bryan.—1st ed.
p.   cm.
"A Jean Karl book."
Summary: In this retelling of a West African tale, Ma Sheep
Thunder and her impetuous son Ram Lightning are forced to leave
their home on Earth because of the trouble Ram causes.
ISBN 0-689-31836-7
[1. Folklore—Africa, West.   2. Lightning—Folklore.
3. Thunderstorms—Folklore.]   I. Title.
PZ8.1.B838St   1993
398.26'0966—dc20
[E]   92-40509

For my *great* niece,
ASHLYN DENNY,
and
to the memory of a *great* friend,
MAUREEN HAYES

A long time ago, I mean a long, long time ago, if you wanted to pat Lightning or chat with Thunder, you could do it. Uh-huh, you could! Thunder was a mother sheep, and Lightning was her son, a ram.

In those days Thunder and Lightning didn't live in the sky, uh-uh! They lived right here on earth. Their home was in a village on the west coast of Alkebu-lan. Uh-huh, Alkebu-lan, called Africa today.

Ma Sheep Thunder and her son lived in the hut where he was born, just east of the marketplace. You'd see them standing by the door of their hut. You could stop for a chat or to pat or just wave as you walked on by. They watched the flow, the come and the go, of the people from the country, the people from the town. When they tired of looking one way, they could always turn around.

"Use your head, Son," Ma Sheep Thunder said. "If things don't work out one way, try another. Hear what I say! I'm your mother."

"I hear you, I hear you!" said Son Ram Lightning.

And he did . . . in his own way.

Ma Sheep Thunder was a good friend of Rain. If the farmer's fields needed moisture, Ma Sheep Thunder would go high up onto the nearby mountain to call Rain. But often she had to call a long time before Rain came.

After her son was born, Ma Sheep Thunder taught him to help her call for Rain. Then her rumbling voice and the flash of her son's fleece, as he raced in the mountain, caught Rain's attention at once, and Rain came quickly.

One season the farmlands were dry. The King sent for Ma Sheep Thunder and Son Ram Lightning. He knew that they were Rain's best friends. They could call Rain down. It took the two of them, he knew it, and he was proud that they could do it. He said,

Crops are thirsty
Land is dry
Call friend Rain
Down from the sky.

Off they went. When they were high up in the mountain, Son Ram Lightning bolted ahead of his mother. He zigzagged across the slopes, sparks flying from his coat. Ma Sheep Thunder followed, calling, "Baa-ba-lam, baa-ba-lam!"

Suddenly rain clouds appeared along the path to the mountaintop. When Son Ram Lightning saw friend Rain in the clouds, he flashed a greeting. Ma Sheep Thunder clapped, "Baa-ba-lam!" Friend Rain stepped out of the clouds and fell.

The villagers cheered. Their crops were saved. They sang and danced in the rain. It is no wonder that Ma Sheep Thunder and Son Ram Lightning were the two most honored inhabitants in the kingdom.

Children liked to pat Son Ram Lightning's coat and watch the sparks fly. Ma Sheep Thunder stood by chatting while Son Ram Lightning stood still for the patting. However, he much preferred racing in the mountain, sparks flying, his mother following.

One year Ma Sheep Thunder and Son Ram Lightning came often at the King's call for rain. The crops were splendid, and there was a great harvest celebration.

The King entered the village in a procession led by the drummers.
People crowded around him.

"Stay right by me," Ma Sheep Thunder said to her son. "Your
horns may have grown out, but you're not grown up yet."

Son Ram Lightning wanted to show off his horns to the King. He and his mother were far back in the crowd. While his mother chatted, he hopped and he jumped, but the crowd blocked his view.

"If things don't work out one way, try another," he said, remembering his mother's words. "Use your head!" He lowered his head, pawed the ground, *parrom, parrom, parrom,* and charged!

With a biff, bam, butt he sent people flying or falling to both sides. It got him to the head of the crowd, uh-huh, it did! He stopped before the King.

"What a hard head," cried the King. "What horns!"

"And they're not all grown out yet," said Son Ram Lightning.

"You boast?" said the King. "It is an outrage at your age to go on such a rampage!"

"I used my head as I heard Ma say. With a biff, bam, butt I cleared the way."

"There is a better way, Son, to use your head," said Ma Sheep Thunder. "Whatever you do, no more biff, bam, butts out of you!"

"There is a proverb," the King said. "A frisky child knocks his face against the rock! Uh-huh! Bad ways will get you into trouble. My people are no rock for your son to knock. To protect them I must move you from the center of the village to the edge of town."

After they moved, Ma Sheep Thunder kept a close watch on Son Ram Lightning, especially when they went to market. For a good while, she kept him out of trouble.

One very hot day, they set out for the village market. It was a long walk. When they arrived in the marketplace, Son Ram Lightning was hungry.

"We'll eat soon," his mother said. She stopped to chat with a friend who made straw baskets and straw hats. As she chatted she soon forgot about food and she forgot about her son.

Son Ram Lightning waited. He grew hungrier and hungrier. Leaning over, he licked a basket. Tasty straw, he thought. He tried another. He licked his way down the line of baskets. Then he started on the straw hats. His teeth nicked a brim.

"A tasty hat," he said. He took a bite. It stirred his appetite. "Um-yum! a delight!" He began munching and crunching the straw hat. He was so hungry, he devoured it and started on another.

Son Ram Lightning didn't notice that this hat was at the bottom of a pile. A few bites into it, and a mountain of straw hats came tumbling down around him.

"Eh, eh!" cried the straw maker when she turned and saw what was happening. Son Ram Lightning was surprised to find himself in a sea of hats. The straw maker raised her broom to strike.

Son Ram Lightning shook free of the hats. He lowered his head and pawed the ground, *parrom, parrom, parrom.*

"Stop!" cried Ma Sheep Thunder.

Whether her "Stop!" was for the straw maker or for her son, it didn't stop either one of them. Son Ram Lightning charged, wham, biff, bam! His head split the broom and spilled the straw maker. She landed, *crunch,* on five straw baskets!

Ma Sheep Thunder helped the straw maker to her feet. She apologized to her friend as she hurried her son away from the scene.

"Didn't I tell you no more biff, bam, butts?" she said.

"That was no biff, bam, butt," said Son Ram Lightning. "That was my wham, biff, bam! I saw that broom coming. I couldn't dodge it, so I charged it. I used my head, just as you said."

"There is a better way for you to use your head, Son," his mother said. "Whatever you do, no more wham, biff, bam out of you!"

When this incident was reported to the King, he sent for the mother sheep and her son ram.

"You're good for rain," he said, "but I'll have to move you once again, even farther away than before."

"We're already at the edge of town," said Ma Sheep Thunder. "How much farther can we go?"

"I'll move you beyond the village," said the King, "past farmlands and fields, to the center of the forest."

"From the center of the village to the center of the forest," sighed Ma Sheep Thunder.

Their new home was a long way off. Ma Sheep Thunder missed the chatting. Son Ram Lightning didn't miss standing still for the patting. He was free now to skip and bound in the forest. His mother didn't have to follow him about all the time. He felt grown up, uh-huh! He could come and go now all by himself.

One morning Son Ram Lightning went out to play.

"Remember now, don't go too far away," said his mother.

After a few bounces and bounds around the hut, he began to bite berries on the bushes nearby. Before he knew it, he had nibbled his way to the edge of the forest. He looked up. There was Ox, eating the vegetables in the field!

Son Ram Lightning knew he was not to leave the forest without his mother. Still, he wanted to save the farmer's crop.

Ma says no biff, bam, butts, he thought, and no wham, biff, bams either. I'll just biff, bop him. That will stop him. Everyone will thank me.

Son Ram Lightning pawed the ground, *parrom, parrom, parrom*. He lowered his head and charged. Biff, bop, he struck Ox from behind.

Ox reared up and cried, "Moorow!" He spun around and came down facing Son Ram Lightning. One look at Ox, and Ram's charge plan changed. He turned and took off.

Son Ram Lightning ran so swiftly that sparks showered from his coat. The sparks caught among the dry leaves. In a short while, flames had consumed more of the farmer's crop than Ox could have eaten in a whole day.

Ox stopped and backed up before the flames. Son Ram Lightning entered the forest. He slowed down when he saw that Ox no longer followed.

By now the villagers had reached the edge of the field. Drummers drummed the fire signal as the villagers cried, "Who fires the field fires food! Friends of Rain should do us good!"

Ma Sheep Thunder smelled the smoke and heard the commotion. She ran out of her hut and caught up with her son.

"To the mountain, to the mountain," she cried. "Baa-ba-lam, baa-ba-lam!"

She called friend Rain as her son streaked ahead. Before they reached the top of the mountain, friend Rain had seen the light flashes and heard the call. Rain came and poured down on the fields until the fires were out.

There was no dancing or cheering in the village this time. A solemn group of villagers stood behind the King as Ma Sheep Thunder and Son Ram Lightning entered the village.

"I've heard the cry of my people," the King said. "They no longer feel safe with you living on earth amongst them. Even when your son tries to help, he hurts. From now on you are banished from my kingdom and from the earth. Your home will be far away from us all, beyond our call, in the sky."

Ma Sheep Thunder and Son Ram Lightning obeyed the wishes of the King and his people. They returned to the mountain. When they reached the mountaintop, they kept on going. They followed the path that clouds take when they come down from the sky to the mountain. Farther and farther along the path they went. At last they reached their new home in the sky. That is where they live to this day.

Every now and then Son Ram Lightning gets away from home.
Uh-huh, he does, and he still causes trouble. He streaks back to earth
and strikes anything in his path. His mother runs after him, her
rumbling voice calling him back. Sometimes Ma Sheep Thunder is
so far behind that we can hardly hear her voice.

Son Ram Lightning hears her, though, but he doesn't always
listen, uh-uh!

I know somebody like that too, uh-huh, I do, but I'm not
saying who.

m lib